And then one goes for a walk,
or a dive in the river!

I have told you so many things!

I'm not used to doing this. I'm usually a guy of few
words who loves silence, but I really loved telling you
about my life!

Telling stories helps one to put ideas in order—
it brings out new ideas and unexpected questions.

But there comes a point at which the story ends,
the place in which you can hear the echo of the words.

I don't know if we capybaras invented this way of being, but I believe that other animals enjoy it too.

Good for them.

Once we become tired of the cuddle clump we
have another way of staying close to each other:
staying by ourselves, but together,
neither too close nor too far.

When we stay by ourselves near each other, loneliness
does not exist. We basically neither see nor talk to
each other, but still we feel connected.

And if we want to, we can also act like tough guys.

The care is guaranteed.

One of my favorite types of care is closeness.

I don't need to explain anything to you about closeness: the next time that you are with your friends or your family, gently clump yourselves together.

Like this, for example.

I'm a capybara, and I'm sure you can see
from my expression that I'm a tough guy.
But not a normal tough guy.

We capybaras know a secret:
tough guys love cuddles and care sometimes.

My friend, the little bird, knows it.

Give me a moment while I drink a bit of it...

And it was the same way with the broth!

Have you ever tasted a food that you thought was no big deal, but you found that it was absolutely delicious?

A well-made broth, for example. One day I happened to taste one and...my goodness, how much I liked it! It's a wonderful potion and magical for one's mood and tummy.

Sometimes I amuse myself with things that I never thought could amuse me.

Sometimes I like things I would have never thought to like.

For example:
once, I put on a bow tie and went to the opera.
Now every time I listen to it, I'm moved.

Everybody wondered:
does he imagine that under the whale disguise he's not
recognized? Or did he dress up just to make us laugh?

I don't know, but it was funny.

I'm a capybara (you know that, by now) and,
like all capybaras, I have a serious expression,
but I laugh a lot under my bristles.

I remember the day I dressed up as a whale.

I must confess: even though I love diving,
I'm a little lazy.

But sometimes I try to work out, and
I realize that it feels funny:
my paws seem longer, I get warm, my back
tingles, and the smell of nature is stronger.

In the end I'm satisfied that I overcame
my laziness, very satisfied.

Have I told you about my love for water?
Bathing, plunging, swimming underwater!

Capybaras are excellent swimmers. We can
spend hours and hours in the water and we
are able to fall asleep floating.

You won't find a capybara's house far from
a river, a lake, or a pond.

Sometimes I see myself in other animals:
even though we are so different, they could be
like brothers to me.

It happened once with a little bird:
we looked at each other and in that moment understood
each other. I showed him my calmness, he let me listen
to his little wings flutter, and he became one of my
best friends.

I often meet other animals and don't know why I get along with all of them.

Of course I get along better with some animals than with others.

Some animals amaze me and I can't stop observing them.

I like to share.
I like to see the world go by,
to play, to explore, to stroll,
then to rest and look around again.

But I was talking about me.
I'm a capybara, and I love living simply.

I like to observe things and their poetry.
Yes, I love poetry,
even without writing or reading it.

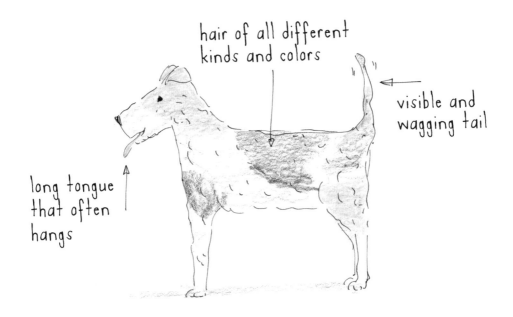

hair of all different kinds and colors

visible and wagging tail

long tongue that often hangs

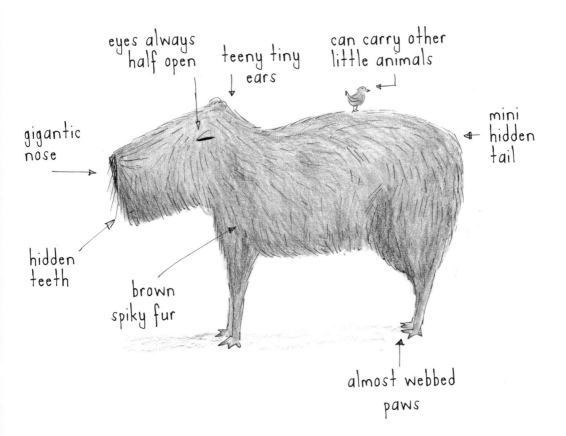

eyes always half open

teeny tiny ears

can carry other little animals

gigantic nose

mini hidden tail

hidden teeth

brown spiky fur

almost webbed paws

Did you think I was a dog?

It's nothing new...

One day at the park I saw a dog that had a rectangular face like mine and I understood that, with enough imagination, one could confuse me for a dog. But while there are many kinds of dogs, we capybaras all look the same.

I must introduce myself because people often mix
me up with other animals.

I'm not a mouse.
I'm not a beaver.
I'm not a bear, nor a marmot.

I'm a capybara, the biggest rodent in the world.

I am a capybara.

Michela Fabbri

I Am a Capybara